Alexander Takes The Bus

Story By – Shaiden Maxwell
Written By – Jurea Maxwell
Illustration By – Ciana Taylor

Alexander, Mom shouted

my name very loudly from the

kitchen. I really did hear her,

but I thought I would put my

head back under the covers

and pretend like I didn't hear

her just so I can get a few

more minutes of sleep. It was way too early for me to wake up. But Mom yelled my name again this time she seemed even louder because she was now in my bedroom. All of a sudden I felt a cold breeze come over my body. Mom had

pulled the covers off of me so

that I could get up and get

ready for school. She said

Alexander it is time to wake

up; you'll be late for school if

you don't get up now.

I growled under my breath and said okay Mommy; I'm getting up now I promise.

Suddenly, I remembered that is was the first day of school and I jumped up out of the bed quickly. I couldn't wait

to meet my new teachers and

hopefully make some new

friends. This year was going to

be different I could feel it.

I will be taking the school bus this year for the first time. I can't wait; this is going to be a great year!

The only thing that sucked was me having to get

up so early every day, ugggh.

I really didn't want to miss the

school bus so I'd have to get

up.

As I was getting dressed

Brady said, hurry up Alex

(Alex is what everyone except

my Mom called me). Oh, yeah

Brady is my parrot. He is

always repeating everything

that I said. Since he always

repeated everything I had to be very careful of what I would say around him because I never knew what he would repeat.

Brady wasn't all bad he covered for me sometimes. I taught him how to say some words like "I don't know" and "it wasn't him". That worked most of the times to get me out of trouble.

It was really funny to me how excited Brady was. He seemed just as excited for me to go to school today; it was almost as if he knew what a special day it was going to be for me.

My Mom and Dad both agreed that I could take the school bus because after all I'm a big boy now. I am eight years old and going to the third grade.

It wasn't like I was the only one taking the bus in the neighborhood. I had my neighbors Nay and Jay who live next door to me. They are twins who go to my school but they are a little older than me.

Nay in Jay are going to the fifth grade this year. They call me their little brother and it is nice to have two older (play sisters) since I was an only child. Also, I had my best friend Max who lives two blocks away from me that is

going to be taking the bus with

us.

   Max and I have known

each other our entire lives.

We did everything together

and now we are taking the

school bus together. I am

happy to have friends that will

be riding the bus with me.

No way was I going to be

scared. Well at least that is

what I kept telling myself. I

sat down to breakfast and

kept saying "don't be scared,

you got this, "don't be scared,

you got this".

Mom had made a very big breakfast. We had bacon, sausage, eggs and grits all of my favorites, however, there was no way I could eat it all.

I have to admit I was a

bit nervous and my stomach

was not going to allow me to

eat like I usually did. I took a

few bites and told my Mom

that I was full; she said that I

could be excused. Just as I

was about to go back to my

room to get my book bag my

Dad stopped me and said, hey

Alex, I replied, yes Dad. He

told me to walk with him so we

could talk. We went and sat

down on the front porch to

have guy talk. I always loved

when we had our talks. He told

me he was so proud of me and

of course he gave me some

rules about taking the school

bus. He said, don't talk to

strangers. Let an adult know if

anyone is bullying you or bothering you. Watch when crossing the street. He also said he loved me and wished me a good day at school. After we finished talking I ran back into the house to get my book

bag because it was getting

late and I couldn't miss the

bus on my first day.

It was almost time for me

to leave and my stomach was

in knots as I heard Brady say

don't be late Alex.

I went back into the kitchen and my Mom gave me the biggest hug and kiss. She handed me my lunch box with my favorite lunch. She had made for me; it was a peanut butter and jelly sandwich, an apple and chocolate milk.

Since the bus picked me up on the corner of my house I didn't have far to go. My Mom grabbed her sweater and her keys to walk me to the corner. In her eyes I was still her baby but I was eight years old now. As we opened the door and began to walk outside we saw the school bus was already at the corner so we had to run to the corner to

catch the bus. Nay and Jay

were already there holding

the bus for me. They were

getting on the bus slowly to

stall the bus driver. They

asked him to wait because

their brother was coming, he

did. The bus driver's name is

Mr. Jake. He is a big man with

a mustache which seems a

little scary, but he actually

was very nice; especially since

he waited for me.

We made it, my Mom waved goodbye and we were on our way to school to start my first day in the third grade. Next stop was to pick up Max; I could see him standing there as we pulled up.

He got on the bus and sat

next to me in the seat that I

saved for him. We joked the

few minutes that it took to

get to school.

I told him this was going to be a good day. Max and I got off the bus and walked into school, we were trying to be cool after all we were third graders now. I can't wait to see how this year goes.

THE END

Thank you to my family for their
never ending support.

Special thanks to my sister Reyne, you're always there for me. You have helped us every step of the way. We couldn't have completed this without you.

Special thanks to Eric, I thank you for your continued encouragement, love and support. You kept me motivated and reminded me that I can do this.

To my son, Shaiden who created the story, I thank you for giving me a reason to write.

To my niece, Ciana for your amazing illustration, thank you for bringing our work to life.

Dedication

To my parents Leroy and Theodora Maxwell, you both are my inspiration and motivation daily. You taught me to never give up and that I can do anything that I set my mind to doing.

Made in the USA
Columbia, SC
11 September 2018